To my Mother.
Your encouragement, nudging, and
belief in me provide inspiration to try new
things and follow new dreams.

With grateful hugs to my daughter, Sarah,
whose faithful hard work has helped me
to complete these illustrations!

Lisa

This story is dedicated to my very special
godchildren and to all my wonderful
family members and friends, most especially
Nicole, Callie, Jamie, and
as always . . . my one and only Queenie.

Mark

A Cricket's Carol

Written by Mark Kimball Moulton ❧ Illustrated by Lisa Blowers

ideals children's books
Nashville, Tennessee

ISBN 0-8249-5488-2

First published in this format in 2004 by Ideals Children's Books

An imprint of Ideals Publications

A division of Guideposts

535 Metroplex Drive, Suite 250

Nashville, Tennessee 37211

www.idealsbooks.com

Previously published by Lang Books, Delafield, Wisconsin

Library of Congress CIP data on file

Printed and bound in Italy

1 3 5 7 9 10 8 6 4 2

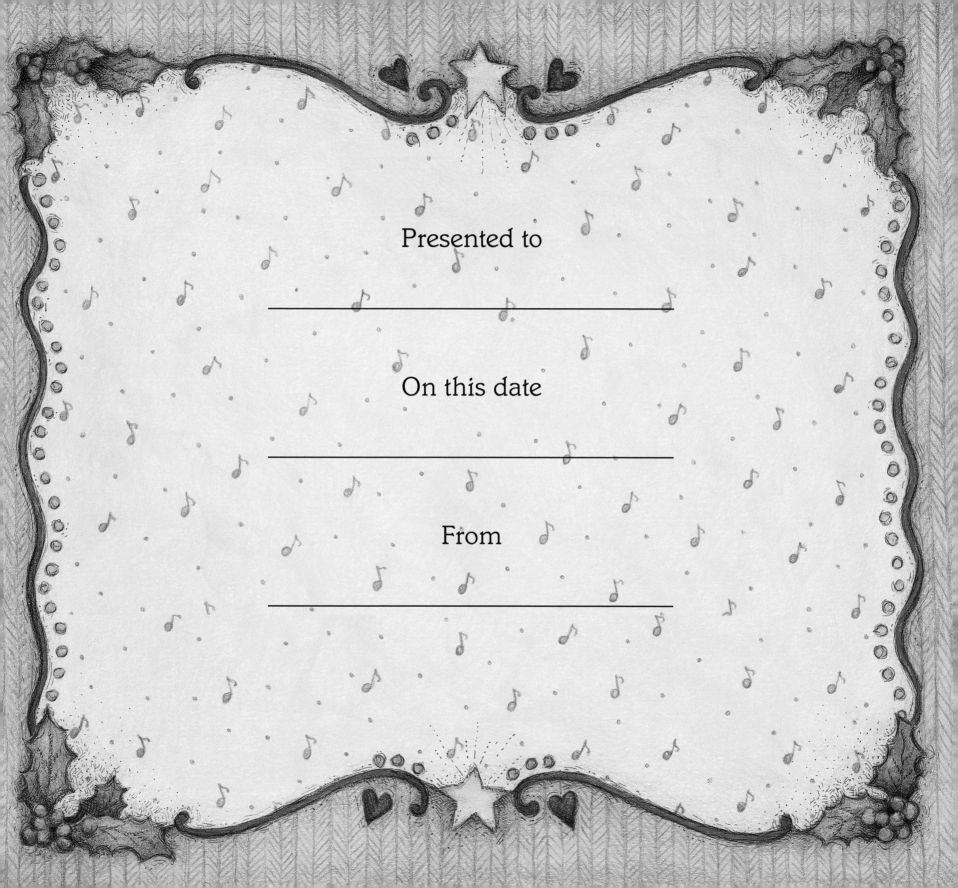

Presented to

_____

On this date

_____

From

_____

any long years ago,
and very far away,
there lived a poor, young orphan boy
named little Toby Grey.

At night he slept in alleyways;
by day he roamed the street,
searching for a crust of bread
or just a bite to eat.

In the bitter cold of winter,
he lit a match for heat
and shared it with the others
who lived along the street.
Toby shivered in his thin, worn shirt;
he had no coat to wear.

With shoes worn through—
and hungry too—
the child was near despair.

Then softly, from a distance
came a carol's sweet reprise,
played upon an instrument he didn't recognize.

A song of light and gentle chords
he hadn't heard for years,
it brought back tender memories
that filled his eyes with tears.

The carol was "O Silent Night"
that little Toby heard.
He soon began to hum along,
not remembering the words.

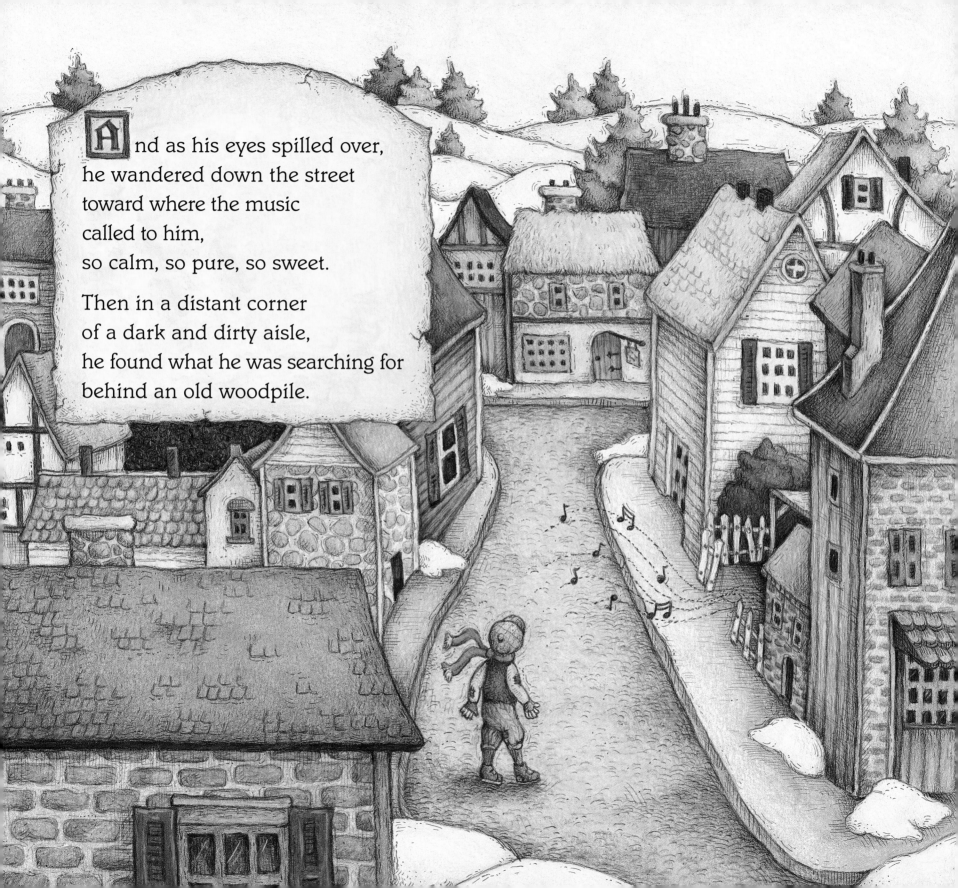

And as his eyes spilled over,
he wandered down the street
toward where the music
called to him,
so calm, so pure, so sweet.

Then in a distant corner
of a dark and dirty aisle,
he found what he was searching for
behind an old woodpile.

He spied a tiny cricket, nearly out of sight,
playing so contentedly, "O Holy Silent Night."

Right beside the cricket,
shiny and brand-new,
Toby found a pair
of hand-stitched leather shoes.

ratefully he put them on,
        as he hummed the cricket's song.
When the cricket played another, Toby hummed along.

Their harmony was lovely,
and folks gathered at their side
to hear the boy and cricket sing their carols of Yuletide.

The Christmas spirit filled the air
as all the crowd rejoiced.
By the time the music ended,
every eye was moist.

And spread all round young Toby,
from folks who'd gathered there,
were gifts of food and clothing—
whatever they could spare.

He shared these gifts with others
who lived upon the street.
And finally, young Toby's friends
all had enough to eat.

When dawn broke that next morning,
a cold wind whipped through the town.
Toby huddled in a doorway,
as wet snow flew all around.

Then, once again, he heard a song—a carol, clear and mild—
played by his friend the cricket,
about Mary and her child.

He searched the streets
and found him,
then felt a warming glow
as he watched the happy cricket
chirping carols in the snow.

Hanging right above him, on a peg stuck in the wall,
was a slightly tattered woolen coat—not a bit too small,
and oh, so warm and cozy.
Toby thanked his tiny friend, for the cricket and his carols
offered comfort once again!

So Toby donned the snuggly coat
against the bitter cold
and hummed and sang those Christmas songs
from very long ago.

And then again, like once before,
a small crowd gathered near
to hear Toby and his new friend
sing "Upon a Midnight Clear."

Kind gifts of food and clothing
meant more to him than gold,
and once again he shared them with
the poor and sick and old.

oon the duet traveled far from noisy city throngs
to entertain the country folks
with heartfelt Christmas songs.

nce, in a cozy bakery,
fragrant with
cakes and bread,
Toby sang with Cricket,
and all the hungry
were fed.

Next, upon a farmer's fence
sat Cricket and the boy,
singing of goodwill toward men, and peace and love and joy.

The farmer loaded baskets
with pumpkins, squash, and more,
and gave them to young Toby to take back for the poor.

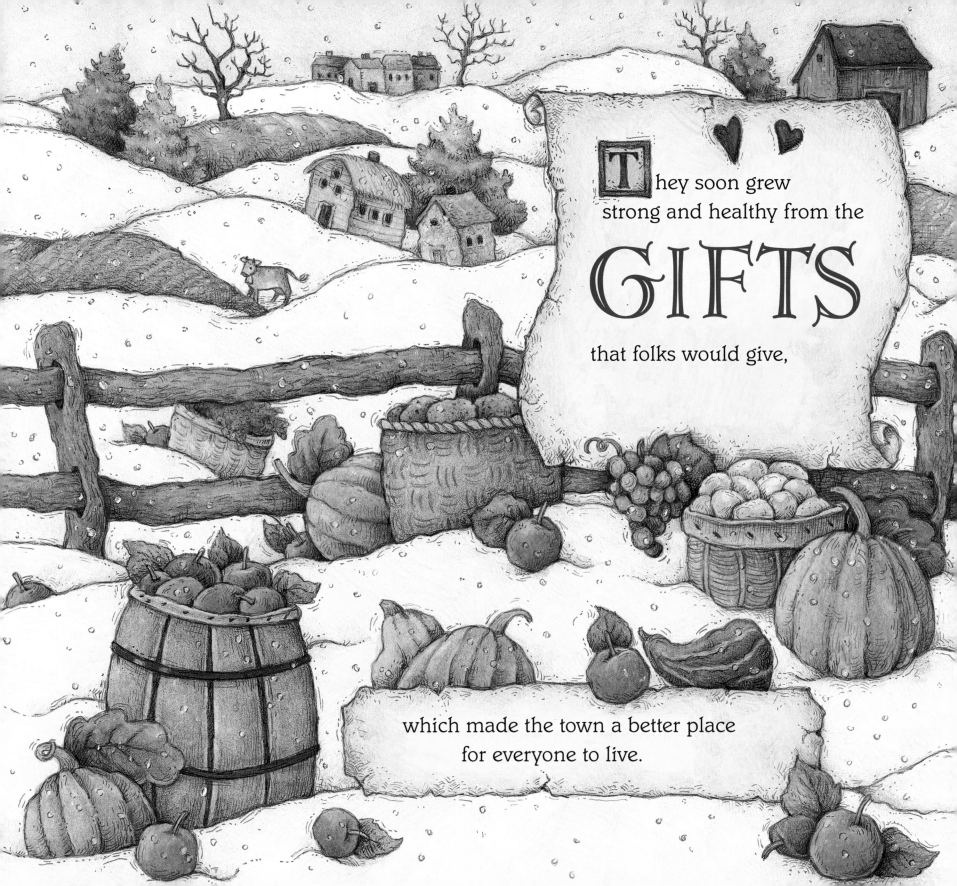

They soon grew strong and healthy from the

GIFTS

that folks would give,

which made the town a better place for everyone to live.

But then one day
the cricket was nowhere to be found.
The forlorn lad looked high and low,
searched the city up and down.

He wandered through the city streets,
more lonely than before,
with fear that he would never see
his cricket anymore.

Then far-off in the distance,
with a sound so clear and pure,
came a melody of Christmas . . .

the CRICKET!

He was sure!

He raced down
the lane
and up a hill,
then came to a quick stop
at a gleaming
snow-white building
with a steeple
at the top.

Toby found the building filled with folks
        and watched a holy play.
There were donkeys, sheep, and three wise men,
        and a baby in some hay.

Candles glowing softly, the room was hushed in awe.
Toby bowed his head and whispered thanks for all he saw.
Then quietly, sweet singing started—carols Toby knew:
"O Little Town of Bethlehem," and "Merry Christmas" too!

Then up in front he saw him—
    the cricket, black and small—
sitting on the manger near the donkeys, sheep, and all.

Toby knew that this was where his little cricket stayed—
    in this church upon the hillside,
    in this quiet village glade.

This must have been how Cricket learned
    the carols that he knew;
he'd learned them while he listened
    from his home beneath the pew!

It made young Toby happy
that his cricket had a home,
and glad to know his friend
would not spend Christmas Eve alone.

He closed his eyes
and made a wish,
for every girl and boy,
that hearts be filled with

HAPPINESS,
GLAD TIDINGS,
LOVE, and JOY!

He thought of all
the special gifts
his cricket friend had brought
and gave thanks
for all these blessings,
as the Christmas message taught.

But still his heart was heavy.
He felt lost and all alone.
What Toby yearned for most
was a family and a home.

Somehow the cricket understood
the orphan's misery.
He knew that all young children
need a loving family.

He hopped down from the manger
and continued down the aisle
and jumped on Toby's shoulder,
which made the dear boy smile.

Later on, the folks outside
    had gathered round the tree,
all holding hands and praying, singing songs of blessed peace.

The world was cloaked in beauty,
    snowy hills rang out with song,
    and Toby soon began to feel perhaps he *could* belong!

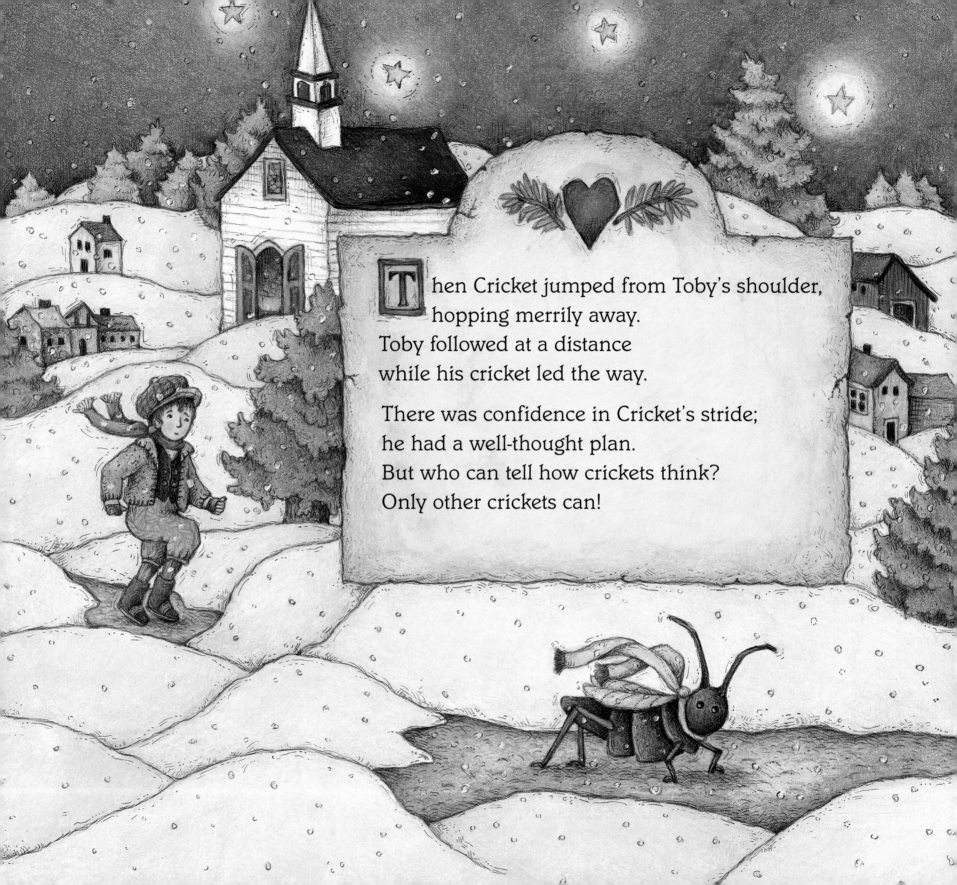

Then Cricket jumped from Toby's shoulder,
hopping merrily away.
Toby followed at a distance
while his cricket led the way.

There was confidence in Cricket's stride;
he had a well-thought plan.
But who can tell how crickets think?
Only other crickets can!

Eventually the cricket's trail
led to a little girl
with a face so kind and sweet—
no dearer girl in all the world.

She asked the boy his name
and wondered where he lived in town.

He told her of his circumstance,
which made her sigh and frown.

He said she shouldn't worry; one thing he knew for sure.
With good health and so many friends,
he really wasn't poor.

They talked awhile,
and in no time
the two became good friends.

Now this is where
our little tale
draws quickly to an end.

For on that day the lovely girl
took hold of Toby's hand.
She brought him to her loved ones—
she knew then he'd understand.
They'd welcome him with open arms.
And so it came to be . . .

That Toby found the greatest gift, the gift of FAMILY.